For Nicola and our beany-seedy thing x

A TEMPLAR BOOK

First published in the UK in hardback and softback in 2012 by Templar Publishing,
an imprint of The Templar Company Limited,
The Granary, North Street, Dorking, Surrey, RH4 1DN, UK
www.templarco.co.uk

Copyright © 2012 by Simon Bartram

The illustrations for this book were painted in acrylics on paper.

First edition

ISBN 978-1-84877-746-0 (hardback)
ISBN 978-1-84877-749-1 (softback)

Edited by Libby Hamilton
Designed by Mike Jolley

Printed in China

Bob
and the
Moontree
Mystery

Simon Bartram

templar publishing

It was a Friday morning in space. Bob, the man on the moon, and his best-ever friend Barry were hard at work giving the dark side of the moon a tip-top tidy up. And that's when they noticed it — a strange beany-seedy thing glowing near crater 1973.

Bob was puzzled. Despite being the world's most brainy moon expert, he had never seen anything like it before. He knelt down to get a closer look. Suddenly, the beany-seedy thing sprang up and briskly bounced away. Bob and Barry looked at each other in astonishment.

Whatever could it be?

Wasting no time, Bob and Barry set off — the chase was on! All afternoon they huffed and puffed until finally the beany-seedy thing jumped deep, deep down into the darkness of crater 483.

By now it was 6.45 p.m., so Bob and Barry had to blast back home quick-sharp or risk missing the big match on TV. Bob wasn't too worried though. After all, what could happen to a beany-seedy thing in just one night?

Back on Earth, Bob couldn't stop thinking about their peculiar discovery. What was the beany-seedy thing doing on the Moon? How did it get there? Some people might have suggested it was the work of aliens, but Bob knew that was just nonsense.

He was still worrying about it the next morning as they rocketed moonwards. All of a sudden, his thoughts were interrupted by an almighty shuddering, shaking crunch! The Moon's surface was still a mile below them.

"We've crashed!" gasped Bob.
"But into WHAT?"

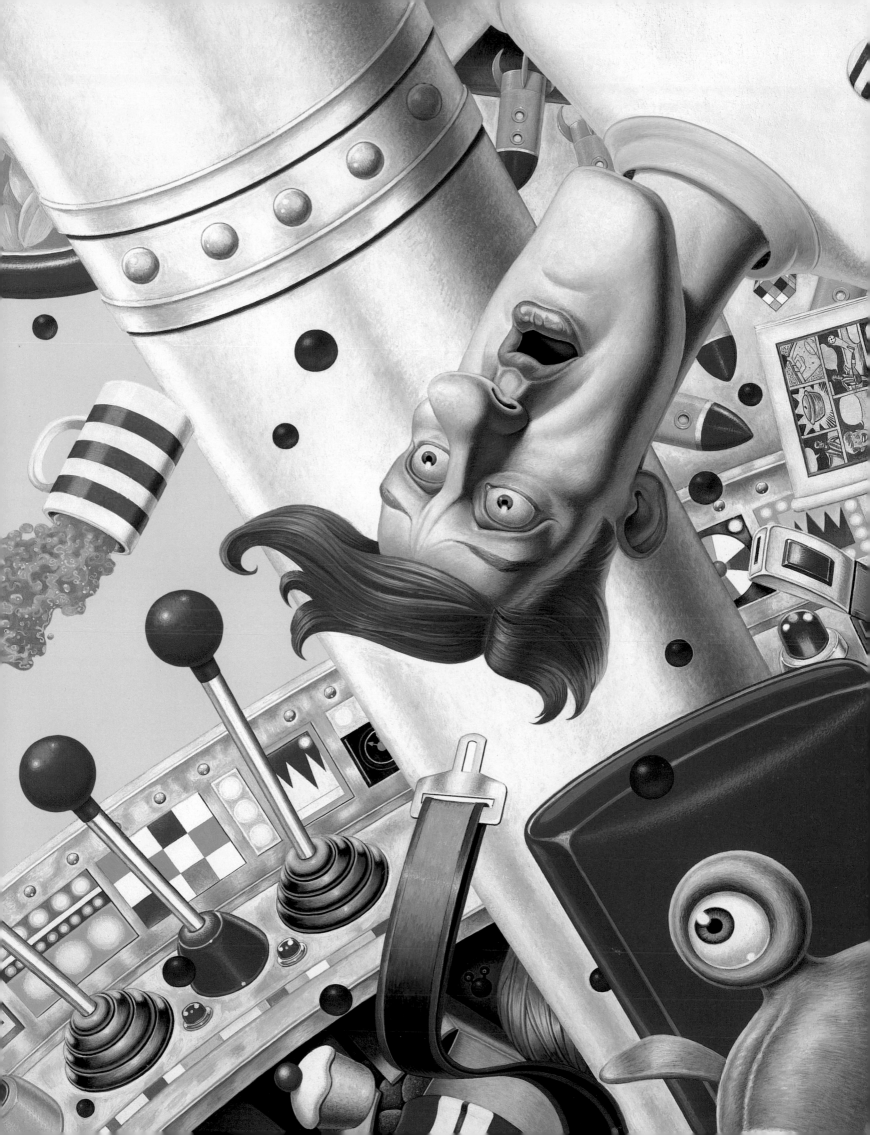

Cautiously, Bob opened the rocket hatch. When he clambered out to see what was what, he was truly amazed. Their rocket was nestled in the branches of a **gigantic, spectacular tree!!**

As tall as a skyscraper, it had shot up directly from crater 483. It was all very odd indeed.

Important questions began to ping around Bob's brain. "A moontree!" he marvelled. "Where could it have come from? And, more importantly, **why is it here?"**

Though still baffled, over the next few days Bob and Barry came to love the Moontree.

It was not only breathtakingly beautiful but tremendous fun too. Bob made a moon buggy tyre-swing and built a tree house where they could enjoy a mini Scotch egg and a bone before their lunchtime game of hide-and-seek amongst the leaves.

Word about the Moontree soon got back to Earth and before long tourists were flocking to see Bob's space chimp impressions and Moontree acrobatics.

Then, one morning, Bob was greeted with another surprise...

The Moontree's branches had sprouted strange golden pod-like berry whatsits! Sparkling between the leaves, they looked mysterious and precious. Bob and Barry gasped at their beauty.

He wasn't sure why, but somehow Bob just knew that the golden podberries were **terribly important!**

News of the golden podberries spread quickly.
Day after day more space tourists arrived,
astounded at the incredible sight.

Many bought souvenirs. Soap-on-a-rope podberries
in particular sold like hot cakes. But Bob had to
explain again and again that the golden podberries
were absolutely not for sale.
No way, no how.

Neither, of course, was the Moontree itself.
Though he still didn't know why it was there,
Bob did know that it was his job to protect it.

And protect it he would.

Each day Bob cleaned and polished every podberry.
Then he would hug the tree trunk as he'd read
somewhere that this was most important.

He cordoned off the Moontree with red rope and
designed a special "hands-off" sign. Unfortunately,
he had missed out an 'o', but he was sure that the
message was still clear.

Under Bob's watchful eye every single leaf and
podberry would be totally safe. The Moontree
was in good hands.

But that night in the tree house, Bob and Barry were rudely awoken by a noisy rustling sound. Suddenly, everything began to shake, slowly at first, then faster and faster, backwards and forwards and side to side.

Bob looked at Barry.

"MOOOONQUAAA

AAAAKE!!"

he bellowed.

Completely helpless, they rattled around the room until, with an enormous **WHOOOOOOSH**, Bob, Barry, the tree house and every last podberry were catapulted away from the Moontree and out into the universe!

Through a thinning sea of podberries, Bob and Barry looked down wide-eyed at the Moon.

A crack had appeared at the base of the Moontree and, as the moonquake continued, the crack grew wider and wider. Finally the Moontree was completely uprooted and it too floated up towards the stars.

In silence, Bob and Barry watched as it glided gracefully past the tree house and disappeared into the distance.

The Moontree was gone.

Bob and Barry were both exhausted. So, in spite of the exciting events of the day, they were soon snoring soundly in the drifting tree house.

Curiously, by the time they woke up there wasn't a single podberry to be seen anywhere. But instead of being upset, Bob was strangely calm. It felt like it was all meant to be.

The tree house sailed aimlessly through space until at last Tony Vanilla's ice cream rocket jingled by. Kindly, Tony gave Bob and Barry a free choc-ice each, then towed them back to the Moon.

The missing Moontree left a big gap in the lunar landscape. Luckily they had no time to feel glum. There was moondust to sweep, leaves to rake and the crack in the moon's surface had to be carefully superglued shut.

When Bob and Barry finally got home to Earth it was late. The drama, however, wasn't quite over.

As they walked up their garden path, something fell out of the sky and plopped into the fishpond. Bob scooped it out at once and couldn't believe his eyes...

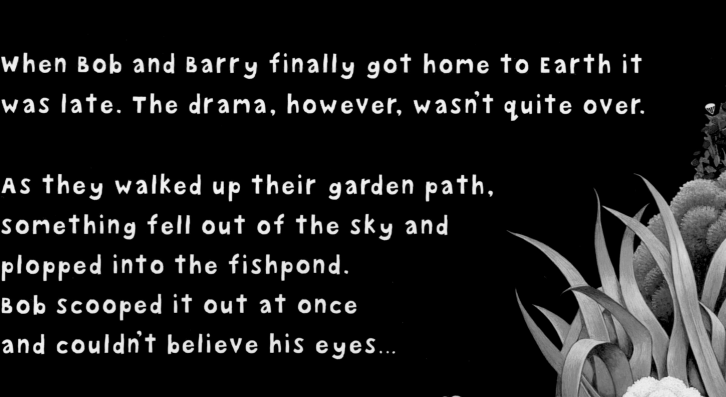

...it was a golden podberry!

From the curl of his quiff to the tips of his toes,
Bob was bamboozled.

As he enjoyed his midnight dippy egg with toasty
astronauts, he wondered what the whole mysterious
Moontree business had been about. None of his
questions had been answered.

All around town there was chit-chat and rumour.
Most people were convinced that aliens had
something to do with the extraordinary events.
But Bob knew that was nonsense. All intelligent
people know there's no such thing as an alien!

"It'll probably turn out to be one of those
great unsolved mysteries of the universe,"
said Bob to Barry as they headed
upstairs to bed.
"After all, if WE can't
work out what's going on..."

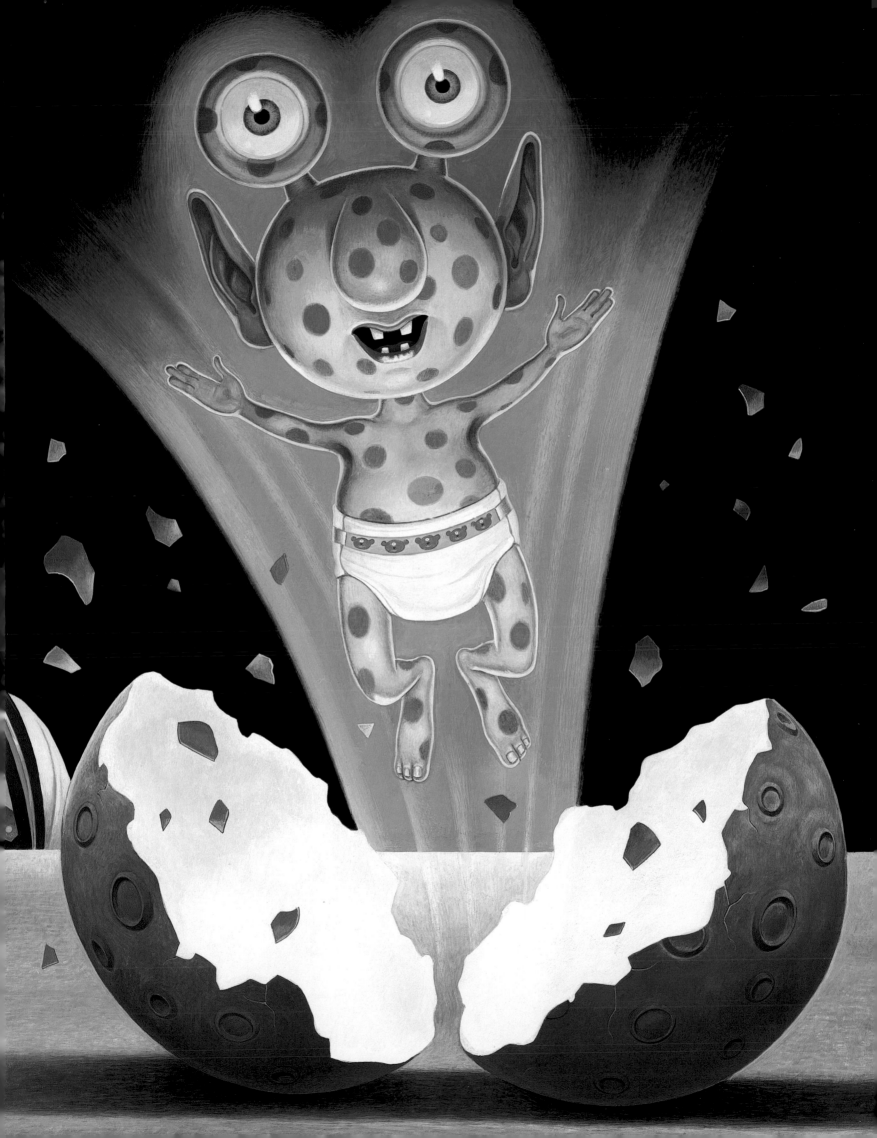